CLAUDE
Dream Bun

BASED ON THE *Alex T. Smith* CLAUDE STORIES
DEVISED FOR TELEVISION BY *Sixteen South*

Hodder
Children's
Books

Claude and Sir Bobblysock were out and about on Claude's bicycle having a jolly time, when suddenly the ride got a little bit bumpy.

"We've got a flat tyre," said Claude.
"But don't worry – I've got just the thing!"

Claude whipped out a bicycle pump from his beret and pumped air into the flat tyre. Soon it was all nice and round once again. "There," said Claude. "All pumped up!"

All the cycling had made Claude hungry.
"Why don't we pop to Mr Lovelybuns' for a nice cup of tea and a slice of freshly toasted raisin loaf?" said Sir Bobblysock.

"Good idea," said Claude.

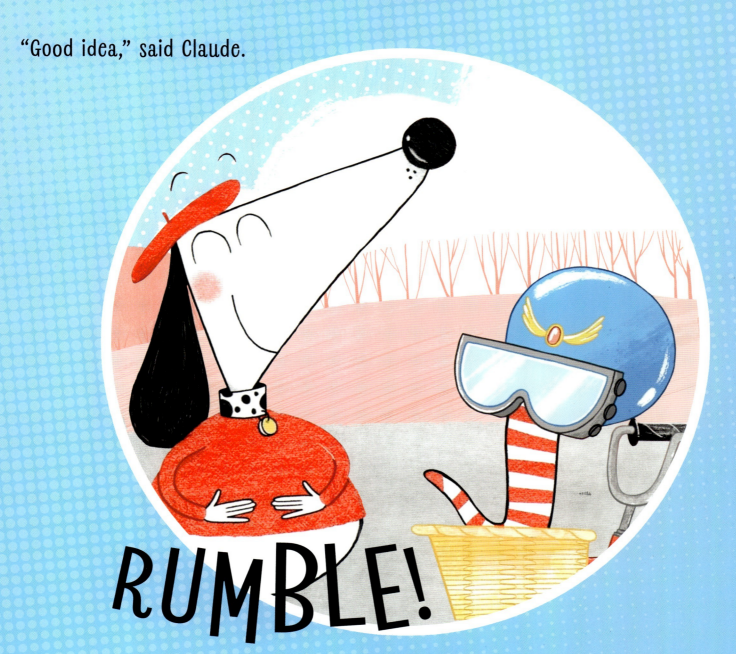

RUMBLE!

When they arrived there was a big crowd bustling about outside.

"I wonder what everyone's waiting out here for," said Sir Bobblysock.
"Let's go inside – I'm starving," said Claude, dashing through the door.

But inside, the café was completely empty!
"Where have all the cakes gone?
And where's Mr Lovelybuns?"
Claude wondered.

"There's not even *one* slice of
raisin loaf," gasped Sir Bobblysock.

"But it *smells* like freshly made
buns," said Claude, sniffing the
air. "Come on, Sir Bobblysock!
Let's investigate!"

Mr Lovelybuns was busy in the kitchen
with a big bowl of bun mix.
"Hello," said Claude. "What's going
on today?"

"I'm trying to break the record for the biggest bun
in Pawhaven history," said Mr Lovelybuns.

Claude's tummy rumbled again.
"That sounds delicious," he said.

RUMBLE!

"It's not for eating," said Mr Lovelybuns. "This bun will be for record-breaking purposes only. To restore the Lovelybuns family name!"

"Whatever do you mean?" Sir Bobblysock wondered.

"Well, my father was a baker. And his father was a baker before him," said Mr Lovelybuns. "They both wanted to bake record-breaking buns, but something always went terribly wrong.

Like the time an elephant sat on grandfather's bun by accident . . .

or when my pop's
bun was swept away
by a tornado up
into the sky."

"But today," concluded Mr Lovelybuns, his eyes gleaming behind his specs, "I plan to put the Lovelybuns name on the record-breaking, bun-baking map once and for all!

If only I had someone to help me," he sighed. "It's such a big job for just *one* baker."

Claude's ears wobbled and his tail waggled . . .

His eyebrows wiggled and he said –

"I CAN DO THAT!"

"You can?" said Mr Lovelybuns.

"Oh, yes!" said Sir Bobblysock, proudly. "Claude knows a *lot* about buns. They're his favourite treat!"

"Oh, thank you, Claude!" said Mr Lovelybuns. "Let's get you an apron."

After a lot of pouring, some careful weighing and a great deal of mixing, the bun mix was popped into the oven and baked to perfection.

"Hooray!" Claude shouted. "It's ready!"

"What a beautiful bun," sighed Sir Bobblysock.
"The biggest bun ever!" said Claude.

"Not quite," sighed Mr Lovelybuns, squinting at his measuring tape. "It needs to be even bigger." He looked ever so disappointed. But Claude had an idea . . .

"When my bicycle got a flat tyre this morning, I pumped it up and it got bigger and bigger and bigger. We could pump up the bun!"

"You can't fill a bun with air," said Sir Bobblysock.

"But maybe we could fill it with something else?" said Claude.

"Why, yes!" said Mr Lovelybuns. "I've got just the thing . . .

My custard-bun-filling machine!"

"Oooh, I *love* custard!" said Claude, his tummy rumbling again.

Mr Lovelybuns jammed the nozzle into the bun and switched the machine on.

RUMBLE!

"It's getting bigger!" cried Claude, as the bun filled up with custard.

"Just big enough!" said Mr Lovelybuns, measuring it up. "Splendid!"

"My big moment! The Lovelybuns family name will be restored at long last!" said Mr Lovelybuns. "You can turn off the machine and take the nozzle out now, please, Claude."

But just then, Miss Hush came in with her important clipboard. "We're all waiting to do the official bun measuring," she said.

Claude quickly wheeled the enormous bun out into the street.

Everyone was waiting to see
Mr Lovelybuns' great big bun.
Claude looked around.
"No elephants or
tornadoes in sight,
Mr Lovelybuns.
Coast's clear!"

Mrs Mayor and Miss Hush measured the bun carefully. They were just about to announce that it was, indeed, the biggest bun in Pawhaven history when . . .

"Ooh! Was that your tummy again, Claude?" said Sir Bobblysock.

RUM

"Not me, Sir Bobblysock," said Claude. "Oh no! The custard-bun-filling thingy! I forgot to take it out!"

BLE!

"Uh oh . . ."
said Sir Bobblysock.

AAT!

"Nooo!" wailed Mr Lovelybuns.
"My dream bun is ruined!"

Mr Lovelybuns was very upset. But Miss Hush wiped the custard off her clipboard and said something that surprised everyone . . .

"CONGRATULATIONS, Mr Lovelybuns! According to the rule book, you've just broken two records. The biggest bun . . . and the messiest!"

"Hurrah! The Lovelybuns family name is restored at last!" laughed Mr Lovelybuns. "I couldn't have done it without you, Claude. Perhaps you'd like to be my full-time assistant?"

"Thank you," said Claude. "But I think I've had enough of buns for now. I might just have a carrot stick instead."

Later on, Claude was curled up in his bed at 112 Waggy Avenue when Mr and Mrs Shinyshoes returned home.

"What's this?" said Mrs Shinyshoes. "It looks like a chef's hat! And are those carrot sticks?"

"Do you think Claude knows anything about them?" said Mr Shinyshoes.

"Don't be silly, dear," said Mrs Shinyshoes. "Claude's been fast asleep all day."

But Claude *did* know something about it. And we do too, don't we?

HODDER CHILDREN'S BOOKS

First published in Great Britain in 2020
by Hodder and Stoughton

1 3 5 7 9 10 8 6 4 2

Based on the original 'Claude' series
published by Hodder Children's Books,
written and illustrated by Alex T. Smith

Storybook text written by Davey Moore

Copyright in images and script for
Record Breaking Bun written by Davey Moore
© 2020 Sixteen South Limited

A CIP catalogue record for this book
is available from the British Library.

ISBN 978 1 444 93870 8

Printed and bound in China

Hodder Children's Books
An imprint of Hachette Children's Group
Part of Hodder and Stoughton
Carmelite House
50 Victoria Embankment
London, EC4Y 0DZ

An Hachette UK Company
www.hachette.co.uk
www.hachettechildrens.co.uk

FSC
www.fsc.org
MIX
Paper from
responsible sources
FSC® C104740